Still Mine

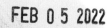

Written by
Jayne Pillemer

Illustrated by
Sheryl Murray

HARPER
An Imprint of HarperCollinsPublishers

Still Mine

Text copyright © 2022 by Jayne Pillemer

Illustrations copyright © 2022 by Sheryl Murray

All rights reserved.

Manufactured in Italy.

www.harpercollinschildrens.com

ISBN 978-0-06-306277-1

The artist used graphite pencil on bristol board and digital color in Procreate to create the illustrations for this book.

Typography by Dana Fritts

21 22 23 24 25   RTLO   10 9 8 7 6 5 4 3 2 1

❖

First Edition

For Grandma Helen—*still mine.*
—J.P.

For all my siblings, with love—especially Sheila,
who is always in my heart.
—S.M.

You are mine in the morning,
when we rise and shine
and sing our song,
tossing kisses to the sun.

You are mine at playtime,
when we swing hand in hand,

letting go and flying
like birds through the air

before our feet hit the sand.

You are mine in the afternoon,
when the sky starts to rain,

and we dance and splash
until the clouds float away.

You are mine at pajama time,
when we share hot chocolate and say,

"Today with you was perfect."
I want tomorrow to be
just the same.

But then you tiptoed by me
and hopped a ride on the breeze.
Now you are gone and I can't come along.
I didn't even get to say goodbye.

What will I do if I don't have you?

Who will sing your sunrise song?

Who will make your special treat?

Who will nuzzle noses?

Who will smooch cheeks?

Can you catch my kisses
if I throw them way up high?

Are you still mine?

When the sun comes up today,
I go to the window by myself.
"Sunshine is a little love from the sky,"
I sing low in the morning light.
It feels soft and warm—like your kiss—
on my face.

Still mine.

At the park, I am sad without you, until I hear your voice in my heart, whispering, "Kindness always helps a smile sprout."

Then I make a friend, and we giggle as I teach her our favorite game.

Still mine.

When storm clouds come,
big and deep dark blue,
I jump and squeal and
stick out my tongue,
just like we used to do.

Maybe *you* sent that rain
to sprinkle some fun on me today.

Still mine.

I miss you most at bedtime—
I miss your stories,
your smooches, your snuggles.

But when I drink my cocoa,
it goes down nice and happy.
It's like a memory inside my mouth,
a little taste of you.

Still mine.

My eyes can't see you anymore;
my arms can't hug you.
But you are always there—
just in a different way.

I can find you in the sun,

in the rain,

in the bottom of my cup.

I can find you in my heart,
because what never goes away
is love.

You are still mine.
Still always mine.